MR. UNIVERSE

MR. UNIVERSE

Arthur Slade

orca soundings

ORCA BOOK PUBLISHERS

Published in Canada and the United States in 2021 by Orca Book Publishers.
orcabook.com

Library and Archives Canada Cataloguing in Publication
Title: Mr. Universe / Arthur Slade.
Other titles: Mister Universe
Names: Slade, Arthur, 1967– author.
Series: Orca soundings.
Description: Series statement: Orca soundings
Identifiers: Canadiana (print) 20200273701 | Canadiana (ebook) 2020027371x
| ISBN 9781459826885 (softcover) | ISBN 9781459826892 (PDF) |
ISBN 9781459826908 (EPUB)
Classification: LCC PS8587.L343 M78 2021 | DDC jc813/.54—dc23

Library of Congress Control Number: 2020939207

Summary: In this high-interest accessible novel for teen readers,
Michael accidentally finds himself in an alternate
universe being chased by scary lizard men in gray suits.

Orca Book Publishers is committed to reducing the consumption
of nonrenewable resources in the making of our books. We make
every effort to use materials that support a sustainable future.

Orca Book Publishers gratefully acknowledges the support for its
publishing programs provided by the following agencies: the Government
of Canada, the Canada Council for the Arts and the Province of British
Columbia through the BC Arts Council and the Book Publishing Tax Credit.

Edited by Tanya Trafford
Design by Ella Collier
Cover photography by Getty Images/Armin Staudt / EyeEm (front) and
Shutterstock.com/Krasovski Dmitri (back)

Printed and bound in Canada.

24 23 22 21 • 1 2 3 4

To all the mad scientists.

And people who feel like they're

stuck in the wrong universe.

One

It was just my luck that my girlfriend lived in another universe.

And, to make matters worse, mysterious gray men were trying to erase her.

My name is Michael, and I'm the last guy you'd think would end up jumping from one world to another. I mean, the closest I'd come to that was playing space-war video games and watching

Marvel movies. But *actually* going from one world to another was way too weird a thing to happen to me.

You've maybe heard of the multiverse idea. Some math and science people figured it out. The idea is that right next to our universe is another universe almost exactly like ours. And next to that is another universe just a pinch different, and next to that is another, and then another. They're kind of like hot dogs laid out next to each other in a pack.

I'm only saying hot dogs because I'm hungry. But it works, right? So let's say I'm from one hot dog, and my girlfriend is from a different hot dog.

Getting from one hot dog to another was considered impossible. It was just an idea those math guys and gals talked about in their fancy classes. They used big words to explain it all.

Then my uncle came along.

He's a super-brilliant math guy. And he's also an inventor. No, his hair isn't crazy like Einstein's or that guy's in *Back to the Future*. My uncle's hair is gone.

He's bald.

And he found out how to jump from one hot dog to another. With a zap.

So he sent me to Earth Two, as I like to call it. Which is *almost* exactly like my Earth.

Earth Two is where I met my girlfriend.

Emily.

Oh, did I mention the gray men who want to erase her?

Two

I know when I call them "the gray men," they don't sound that scary. But they are. You see, not only do they wear gray suits and gray ties, but they also have lizard eyes.

And razor-sharp shark teeth.

You can't see their eyes at first, because they wear sunglasses. The gray men probably don't have souls. They certainly don't have hearts.

And they are really, really dangerous. I did see them erase someone once.

So there's that.

Three

It all started when I went to visit my uncle for the long weekend. He lives in a dome house in the country. There's a smaller dome on top of his house where he has a telescope. He uses it to plot star charts and watch the universe.

Anyway, Mom sent me there because she and Dad Two (that's what I call my stepdad) wanted to go away for the weekend. Without me. Which I was totally cool with. I don't want to see them face-suck each other. It's like watching fish kiss.

But what wasn't cool is they didn't trust me to stay in our house on my own.

Not since that party thing happened. And the police came. Oh, and our garage burned to the ground.

Anyway, they sent me away to Uncle Henry's place.

Mom also said, "Keep an eye on your uncle. Make sure he hasn't gone off the deep end."

So I'm not sure who was looking after who. Or is it whom? I can never remember.

Four

Uncle Henry hadn't gone off the deep end. In fact, he'd gone off the shallow end. That joke will make sense in a second.

When I got to his house, I rang the doorbell and waited. Then I rang it again and waited. No one came to the door. Finally I let myself in.

"Hello! Hello! Uncle Henry?"

I found my uncle in his lab, which looks exactly like one you'd see in those crazy science shows. The room is stuffed full of all sorts of tubes and electrical wires and ancient laptops (probably connected to the dark web). It's a messy, cool place.

"Oh, you're here," he said. "I forgot you were coming this weekend. I'm so bad at temporal things."

"Yeah, me too," I said, even though I wasn't sure what *temporal* meant. "What are you up to?"

He gave me a great big grin and pointed at a weird machine that looked like about twelve computers glued together and then wrapped up with wires. "Well, Michael, you see it's a mixture of *blah, blah, blah* math to come up with the *blah, blah* that would occlude any *blah, blah, blah, blah...*" He went on like that for about five minutes. And none of it made any sense to me at all. He talked a lot like one of those scientists in the superhero movies, and I'm pretty sure he said "quantum" something several times. He pointed at a pan of water on the floor and mentioned that it was "hypercharged" with gamma. "It's a quantum multiverse transporter," he said, as if that explained everything. "It uses heavy water."

That's what I meant earlier when I said he'd gone off the shallow end. It was a shallow pan of water.

"It's great to see you, Michael," my uncle said. "Thanks for listening to your crazy ol' Uncle Henry. I'm pretty busy, but the house is yours. You can do anything you want—watch TV, eat cereal, look out the telescope." Then he pointed at the round pan of water on the floor. "Just don't step in that pan."

"Okay, I won't," I said.

Five

I stepped in it.

But not right away. Because Uncle Henry was so busy, he said what adults often say to teenagers. "Go upstairs and find something to eat. Check the expiry dates though. And don't drink my beer."

I was starving, so I took him up on his offer. I went upstairs. His home is like a toy store. There are miniature robots and model spaceships and those

Star Trek figures. I mean the really old *Star Trek*, the one that was on TV back in the sixties. And he had things from even older shows too.

He had nothing from *Star Wars* though. He said they didn't do their math or science research right. The explosions were a joke, he said. Don't ever watch a space movie with him. He'll wreck it. He presses *Pause* every few minutes and explains why things don't explode into flames in space. Or how gravity doesn't work that way. Or after a really cool fight scene, he'll stop the movie and say, "There's no way to turn a spaceship without side burners."

He has ruined many movies for me.

Anyway, I checked the fridge and started pigging out. There was an entire chocolate cake in there! With chocolate icing an inch thick. There was already a slice missing, so I figured that meant the rest of the cake was up for grabs.

I'm not a barbarian. I only ate half of it. But then my guts started to hurt. I needed a drink. Uncle Henry is a Dr. Pepper freak. He says it's the only doctor he trusts except for Dr. Who. I don't really get that joke, but I sucked back almost a whole one of those really big bottles of Dr. Pepper. I got a really great sugary high for about thirty seconds. And then my stomach began to rebel. It felt like I had swallowed a cannonball. I ran to the bathroom but couldn't find any antacids. I put my headphones on and cranked up my music, hoping that would take my mind off the giant lump in my stomach. But even the fine tunes didn't fix it.

I stumbled back down to my uncle's lab to ask if he had anything that would help. He had his back to me. He was welding something. I didn't want to interrupt, but my stomach was burbling and gurgling. This was urgent.

As I rushed up to him, I stepped in that pan of water.

In the "heavy" water.

My uncle turned around when he heard me say, "Oh crap."

Except I didn't use the word crap. Uncle Henry whipped off his welding mask. He was about to give me a lecture on suitable language, but then he got a really, really scared look on his face.

Scared for me, that is.

"Don't move, Michael!" he shouted. I kept perfectly still. "I'm going to shut down the quantum generator, and everything will be peachy keen."

I got all tingly.

"I said don't move," he repeated.

But I got really, really, really tingly. Like every one of my molecules or cells was vibrating.

Six

For a couple of seconds there wasn't a thing in front of me. Nothing at all. Just blackness. It felt like I was standing on nothing.

Then I was suddenly in sunlight and on pavement. I was in the middle of a street.

And a three-wheeled car was coming straight at me.

The car's brakes squealed, and the driver swerved by me. He shouted, "Garb flabbing grat!" And he shook his fist at me and kept going.

I sucked in a deep breath. And another and another and another. I thought I was dreaming!

But my socks and shoes were still wet from the water in that pan. The pan and everything else was gone. I stared down at my feet.

I heard an odd, trumpet-like honk. Another three-wheeled car was charging down the road toward me. I jumped out of the way and rolled onto the sidewalk.

The car whizzed by, horn honking. The woman driving didn't yell at me though.

I'd never seen a three-wheeled car before, and now I'd seen two in a row. Weird.

It was weird because cars are my hobby. The only three-wheeled cars I knew of were in Japan and Britain. Maybe the ones I'd just seen were a new type of electric car. They hadn't made very much noise. Or maybe a three-wheeled-car convention was in town. But I would have heard about that.

When the third three-wheeled car whizzed by, I started to freak out.

I walked down the sidewalk, trying to get my bearings. The buildings around me looked a little bit familiar, but I couldn't place exactly where I was. I mean, it looked like my city, but Kingston is big enough that I don't know every part of it.

I figured I must have blacked out in Uncle Henry's lab. Maybe I had been electrocuted and had gone straight into a coma.

And now I was awake. Or not. Nothing was making sense.

If this was real, how had I gotten here? In the middle of the street?

My uncle wouldn't have put me here. He was usually nice to me.

Ah! I nearly put my finger in the air as I walked. Uncle Henry must have called an ambulance. It had been racing really fast to the hospital. It had hit a bump and the door had opened, and I'd fallen out. And the driver hadn't noticed and had kept on going.

That had to be it.

I just needed to find the nearest hospital. Or call my uncle. I dug out my phone from my back pocket. It had a cracked screen from the time I had been showing off my juggling skills, but it still worked.

No service.

Huh. So I continued down the sidewalk, still feeling that sugar high.

And that's when I saw her.

Seven

Actually, what I saw was a blue blur as a girl ran past me, her ponytail bobbing. As she did, she shouted, "Hurry up, you garb flabbing grat! We're going to be late."

She sounded confident and a bit like she knew me, so I decided I had better listen to her. I started to run after her.

After a couple of steps she turned and said, "Oh. You're not Mick."

"No, I'm Michael," I said, and I wondered for a moment if she was going to scream, *Stalker! Stalker! Stalker!*

But she just grinned and said, "Hi. I'm Emily. Sorry for calling you a garb flabbing grat."

"Well, no one has ever called me that before," I replied, just as I remembered how the first driver to almost run me over *had* shouted those words. I figured they must be some sort of cool new swear words the kids were using.

"Oh, I get called it all the time," Emily said. "Well, we better hurry up or we're going to be late. For a very important date."

The word *date* made me nervous. It always does. My palms began to sweat. Were we already on a date? I mean, not that I minded.

"What are we late for again?" I asked.

"School, of course," she said. Then she laughed. "Oh, I get it. You were joking. Ha! Good sense of humor."

Most people don't tell me I have a good sense of humor. But she hadn't sounded sarcastic when she said it.

"Yeah, school," I said. "How could I forget?"

I saw a great big brick building just a block away. It was a school called Max High. I didn't recognize it, but I'd given up on figuring out exactly where I was. I was beginning to believe that the chocolate cake I'd stuffed myself with had affected my brain. Had somehow made me forget the last day and a half.

"It's the first day of classes," Emily added.

I'd already been going to school for almost two months. This had to be a private school. They could start and stop whenever they wanted to. "Oh yeah, right," I said.

She gave me a look and then opened the door for me.

So I went into the school. Why not? I said to myself. Maybe this would turn into an actual date.

Two men in gray suits were standing against the wall. I could see our reflections in their sunglasses. They made me feel uneasy, though I don't know why. They turned to look at us. One of them lifted something like a phone, but it was a triangular shape and not rectangular. I guessed they were security guards about to scan us. And for some strange reason I wanted to throw myself between Emily and them. But just then a group of students walked between us and the gray men. We slipped away.

I followed Emily into a classroom. I glanced back and saw that the gray men were pointing their triangle at other students.

I sat behind Emily, and she said, "Don't be shy. Sit with me."

So I did.

The teacher at the front of the room had already started talking—about mining the second moon. I assumed this was some kind of science-fiction class. I listened as hard as I could, but the scent of Emily's perfume drifted into my nostrils. I tried not to breathe it in too obviously. But it smelled nice. Like cinnamon.

When the teacher was done talking about the second moon, Emily pulled out her phone and checked the time. I noticed her phone was round— I'd never seen that type before. "Whoa, we really were late," she said. "It's almost lunchtime. Do you want to have lunch with me, Michael?"

"Yeah, sure," I said. "But I didn't bring anything to eat."

"Yeah, no kidding. You don't even have a back-pack. You pack light, Michael. So tell me, Michael, do you like sandwiches?"

"I love 'em," I said. It was true. I will eat every type of sandwich. Even egg salad.

"Cool. I'll share mine with you."

We went out to the school courtyard and sat on stone benches. Other students walked by. No one I recognized. Emily waved at one and pointed at her ear as if to say "call me," and then she brought out her sandwich bag. She gave me half a sandwich.

"Turkey," she said.

"Huh?" I replied, thinking she was calling me a name.

"It's a turkey sandwich."

"Oh. Thanks! Thanks." And I took a bite to shut my silly mouth. It was the best bite of turkey sandwich I'd ever had. I could have eaten that sandwich all day.

But it only took me about five seconds to finish it.

I saw a bus pull up. It was yellow like all the school buses I've seen. But it had just three wheels. Two at the back. One at the front.

"Oh, you were hungry," said Emily. "So tell me, Michael. Are you new at the school? I've never seen you before."

"I think I'm new everywhere," I said. Some of my uncle's big words were coming back to me now. Like *quantum multiverse transporter*. I was pretty sure he'd said something like that. And I was pretty sure I'd stepped into the transporter.

"New everywhere?" Emily said. "Well, I don't know what that means, Michael. But I do like to help out the newbies. I'm kind of a newbie myself."

"I-I wonder...which city is this?" I asked.

"Are you *that* new?" And she backed away from me a bit, like I was crazy. "It's Kingston."

"Oh, good," I said. "I'm from Kingston."

"Of course you are," Emily said. "That's why you go to school here."

"I was beginning to think I was from someplace far away."

"You're a strange dude," she said. It didn't sound like she meant that as an insult. Then she pulled out her round phone again.

"Where'd you get that phone?" I asked. "I've never seen one like it."

"Well, now you're being really strange, Michael." She waved the phone at me. "This is a uPhone. Everyone has one." She ran her finger around its edge, and the screen came alive. "Did you grow up in a cult? Or are you homeschooled?"

"What? No!" I said. Then I took out my iPhone.

Her eyes grew really, really big. "Whoa!" she said. "I've never seen a rectangular phone before."

"It's all I've ever seen. You can fit it right in your pocket."

Her eyes grew even wider. "Pocket?"

Which is when I noticed she didn't have pockets on her jeans. She did have a round purse though.

"I think I know what's happening," I said.

"What?" she asked.

"I think I'm from a different universe."

Eight

Emily stared at me for a full five minutes. Well, it was probably five seconds, but it felt like a really, really long time. My uncle had told me not to step in that pan of water. He'd said it was heavy water. Don't they use heavy water for those atomic bombs? He'd also said it was a transporter. And now here I was, with a girl with a round phone and in a place where the buses and cars only have three wheels. And there are two moons.

I looked up at the sky, but only the sun was visible.

"You're freaking me out a bit, dude," Emily said. "Is this your sense of humor?"

"Yeah, yeah," I said. "I'm just trying to be funny. Sorry. My mom says my humor is a work in progress."

"My flat mom says that about me too," she said.

Flat mom? What was that? I had an image of a mom who was flat as a pancake. But before I could ask, Emily said, "What's your code, Michael?"

My code? Was she asking for my phone number? I looked at my phone and saw I actually had a single bar of service. "You first," I said.

She started reciting her number, although it actually had some letters in it too. That was weird. But I played it cool and entered them anyway. "Wow, that's an interesting number," I said once I'd entered it in my phone.

"I know. Not many people get the Z in their code. I'm lucky."

I sent her a text.

Hi, Michael here.

That was as clever as I could manage.

A trumpet sounded on her phone. "Got it," she said. Then a second later she added, "Oh, wow. Yours is all numbers. How interesting."

"Yeah," I said. "I guess it is."

She texted back.

Emily, at your service.

So I had a girl's number. Or letter-number. Whatever. And my phone was working. For a second I thought I should phone my uncle. But then I looked at Emily. If this was all a dream caused by eating too much chocolate cake, I didn't want to wake up. Ever.

"So did you grow up in Kingston?" I asked.

"I don't think so," she answered.

"Umm, you don't know?"

"Well, yeah," Emily said. "I mean, I'm not sure. I may have lost my memories."

"All of them?" I asked.

"No. But all of them up until about a month ago. As far as I can remember, I just kind of appeared in Kingston. At the main library."

I knew the feeling. "Were you dressed?" I asked.

"What kind of question is that?" Emily was frowning at me now.

Oops. I realized I should have thought before I spoke. Now she probably figured I was creepy. But really, I was thinking of the *Terminator* movies, where people who went back in time arrived totally naked. And now I was trying hard not to think about Emily naked. I could feel my ears turning red. "I, uh, I mean, did you have everything with you?"

"Oh. Okay. Yes, I was dressed," Emily said. "But no suitcase. And I could remember my first name, but not my last. The police couldn't figure out where I'd come from. They searched up and down the webernet and international missing-persons bulletins. Apparently, no one was missing me."

"Wow," I said. That was all that came out. I was really failing on the clever-reply thing. "What did they do?"

"They put me in a home. They call it a flat. For orphans and such. And I have a flat mom who watches out for me. She arranged for me to go to school here. I met a few of the other people in the flat. Made friends. In fact, one of them is just like me."

"You mean pretty?" Oops. I hadn't meant to say that out loud.

"What?"

Oh no! I was climbing higher on the creepiness scale. "Um. That person looks like you? Like, a sister?"

"No. He doesn't. Actually, he looks a lot like you. His name is Mick." Oh, so that was why she'd called me Mick when she first saw me. "He was found around the same time I was. And he doesn't remember anything about his life either. No one can find his family."

"Whoa," I said. "That's a little freaky."

"Yeah. But anyway, he's really a nice guy."

"Oh?" I said. "Have you dated?" What was wrong with me? "I mean, is he single?"

Emily looked at me for a second before replying. "Why? Did you want to ask him out on a date?"

"No. I mean, are you going out with him? I mean, I'm just curious if the two of you are making friends here. If this is a friendly place. That's all I..."

She laughed. "You look so cute when you blush. But no, Mick and I haven't really been here long enough to make friends. And the kids all look at us like we're strange. My flat mom says it'll just take time. Kingston isn't a big town."

"That is so interesting," I said. "I mean, not the size of Kingston, but the whole story."

"You're funny," she said. "Anyway, I'm sure I'll start remembering things someday. Until then I'll just keep going to school."

"Yeah, school," I said. As usual, I couldn't think of anything clever to say. Better not to try too hard.

The school bell rang.

"What class do you have next?" Emily asked.

"I'm not sure."

"Is it geometry?" she asked.

I nodded. "Yeah, that's it," I said. I guessed I'd be following her to geometry class.

"We better get going then," she said. And she grabbed my hand, just for a second, and pulled me along. Then she squeezed it and let me go.

Oh, wow. Her hand was very warm.

Just then my phone began to buzz. What terrible timing.

I looked down and saw who was calling.

"I'll catch up," I said.

Nine

Uncle Henry's face appeared on my screen. I tapped on it and put the phone to my ear.

"Hello?" I said.

"*Rrrgh rargrgg,*" Uncle Henry said. It was a really fuzzy line. He sounded a bit like a Wookiee. "*Rrggh.*"

"I can't hear you. This is a bad connection."

There was a loud zapping noise on my phone, and I worried something had shorted. Then Uncle Henry again. "Is. That. *RHRGHR*. Better?"

"Yes," I said. "Can you hear me?"

"Yes. *RHRHZ*. Where are you?" Uncle Henry asked. "Is there *RHGR* air there?"

Air? Why would he ask that? "Yes. Lots of air. I'm in Kingston."

"Not your *RHRHS* Kingston," he said, still breaking up. "Are you safe?"

"Yes," I said. I almost added that I had met a girl but decided to keep that to myself. "I ate a turkey sandwich," I said.

"*RRHZ*. Turkey? You're in Turkey?" Uncle Henry seemed to be shouting.

"No. I ate a turkey sandwich. It was really good." I watched Emily walking toward the school building. She looked back to see if I was coming. She waved.

"Food. Good," my uncle said. "Wait! Be careful what you eat. Things are *Rgrrg*."

"Things are *what*?"

"It worked!" he replied, ignoring my question. "It really worked. You're in *RGGHGHF*."

"I'm in what?" I asked.

"I want you to take a deep breath," Uncle Henry said. I heard him take a deep breath. "Michael, you've been transported to another Earth. Another universe. Let's call it Earth Two."

"Yeah, I know," I said.

"You do?" He sounded surprised that I had put two and two together.

"Yeah. I figured it out. It took a while," I said, "but then I was like, cool. Congrats on your experiment working."

"Thanks," he said. I could hear the smile on his face. "I'm very pleased. But…umm…don't tell your mom. She'd be mad."

"I won't tell her," I said.

"I didn't mean to send you. I was going to send myself. But…well…tell me about it. How is it different from Earth One?"

I looked out at the street. "Well, all the cars have three wheels, the phones are round, and the people here swear differently."

"I see, I see," he said. I imagined he was writing down everything I said. "Now don't worry, Michael, I'm working on getting you back. I just haven't found the right quantum loop yet."

"Oh, you're going to bring me back." I hadn't really thought that far ahead. I was surprised by how disappointed I felt. I mean, I had to go back, right? "That's good. I guess."

"It's going to take some time," said Uncle Henry. "It's complicated. First of all, I have to restart the quantum generator. It's like firing up a Model T."

"I understand. Don't rush. It's important to get it right." Maybe Emily and I could go to a movie. Even another turkey sandwich would be great. Could I count that as a lunch date?

"Whatever you do, don't *RGHGhR*," he said.

"What?" I said. The line was going all fuzzy again. "Don't do what, Uncle Henry?"

"*RGGHG*. And watch out for *RGHGH*!" He was shouting again. "They have lizard eyes. And the *RHGHS*. Okay?"

Did he say *lizard eyes*?

Suddenly the line went dead. "Uncle Henry? Uncle Henry?"

I put the phone in my pocket. Don't do *what*? I wondered. I started to jog toward the school. I was pretty sure Uncle Henry hadn't said, *Don't go to geometry class and sit with a girl*. In fact, he'd probably be happy to hear I was doing that.

He's a big fan of geometry.

I ran, worried Emily would disappear into a classroom before I could find her. I opened the door and looked left and right. There were tons of students with backpacks on, marching up and down the hallways.

Emily had vanished.

Ten

I wouldn't have found Emily if not for the smell of french fries. I was jogging up the hallway, stopping at each door and peeking in like a spy. Except for the girls' washroom. I didn't want to get arrested.

I could have just waited outside until Emily's class was over. But I was feeling super nervous, and not just because of the stuck-in-an-alternate-universe thing. I had a gut feeling that something had happened to her.

My uncle had tried to warn me about the dangers on Earth Two. I wished I knew what he meant about lizard eyes. Just thinking about it made me jittery.

Then I smelled the greasy deliciousness of fries. As I floated toward the kitchen, I glanced into an empty classroom next to it. There was Emily. And she was holding some guy's hand and pulling him like she really wanted him to go with her.

Oh jeez. So much for going to the movies with her. She'd already found someone else. My heart felt like a melted chunk of cheese.

It took me a second to realize that Emily looked angry. Really angry. Maybe she was trying to get away from this guy.

My temper flared. I burst through the door and shouted, "Unhand her!" I sounded very old-fashioned. I have no idea where that came from.

But opening the door gave me the full view. Now I could see that there were two men in gray suits and dark sunglasses in the room. One of them was holding the guy's other hand. I could tell by his face that he was not going to let go.

"Oh, wait, unhand *him*!" I shouted.

"Yeah, let Mick go!" Emily shouted.

So this was Mick! He had dark hair like mine, but I was pretty sure he was at least an inch shorter than me.

The second man held a square black device in his hand. It looked like a fancy flashlight. He pointed it at Mick.

"He weighs too much," the man with the device said. Then he pressed a button.

A green beam of light came out of the thing. And suddenly Mick was gone. Like, *erased* gone.

It's hard to explain. It all happened so fast. I think the man waved the device up and down. The beam, which was about a foot wide, made part of

Mick vanish. It wasn't gory, like he'd been cut in half. There wasn't blood or guts or anything like in the movies. Half of him was just gone. *Poof!* Mick stared down at his missing half with his mouth open like he was about to scream.

And then the gray man erased the other half of him.

Now Mick was gone. All gone.

With nothing to hold on to, Emily fell over.

I thought she'd start screaming her head off. I know I wanted to. I mean, Mick had just vanished. There wasn't even smoke or anything. But Emily launched herself to her feet, pointed at one of the gray men and said, "What did you do to him?"

"He weighed too much," the man said, shrugging. "His weight was causing an imbalance." Then he pointed the square thing at Emily. "You weigh too much too," he said. "Adjustments are required."

Emily lifted an eyebrow and grit her teeth. It was clear she was getting very, very angry.

"What the garb flabbing grat do you mean?" she asked, glaring at the man.

"The balance must be restored," he said. "It is the way of things."

Then he lifted his flashlight eraser thing. I knew her anger wouldn't prevent him from erasing her too.

So I jumped at him. Just like in the movies, I launched my whole body into the air and slammed into him. Well, that's how I thought it would play out.

What really happened is that I slipped and hit a table with my shoulder, and then the table knocked over both gray men. Just like I'd planned.

I grabbed Emily by the hand and pulled her out of the room.

"But what about Mick?" she asked. She looked like she was in shock.

"It's like he was erased. I don't know. But I do know we need to get out of here—now."

Both gray men were on their feet by the time we reached the door. One of them pointed that black thing right at me. He said calmly but loud enough for me to hear, "You weigh too much too."

How rude. We raced out the door.

Eleven

We ran down the hallway and around the corner. Ooof! We ran smack into a short, stocky woman with a grumpy look stamped on her face.

"Principal Harker!" Emily shouted. "There are men chasing us! They're armed!"

"Hold it!" commanded Principal Harker. She put up a meaty hand. She looked strong enough to arm-wrestle Bigfoot. "Slow down. No running in the hallway. Wait. What did you say?"

Emily repeated herself. Then she looked over her shoulder. The men in gray suits had come around the corner and were approaching us now. They weren't running. They were just moving slowly and confidently toward us. It was super creepy.

"Right there!" Emily pointed. "That's them."

"She's right!" I echoed. "And they are armed. They have a flashlight eraser gun."

I knew how stupid that sounded as soon as I said it.

Principal Harker looked at me. She frowned. "And you are…?"

"I'm Michael," I said. "I'm…I'm a new student. But who I am is not important right now. Look!" I pointed. The men were only twenty feet away now. But somehow their legs weren't moving. They weren't walking so much as floating toward us.

"You should call the police," Emily said. "They melted Mick."

"I should call the counselor is what I should do." Principal Harker looked down the hall and then back at us. "There's no one else here but us three."

"What do you mean?" I asked.

I could clearly see the gray men. Their reflective sunglasses were freaking me out. The closest one smiled, and I could see that his teeth were very, very sharp. I shivered. "They're right there!"

"Can't you see them?" Emily asked. She sounded calm. I felt like screaming at the top of my lungs. "They're the ones who erased Mick."

"There is no one there," Principal Harker said. "No one. And what do you mean, *erased* Mick?"

"Poof! Vanished," I said. I snapped my fingers. "Just like that."

"This is a really juvenile attempt at a prank," Principal Harker said. "And I'm not in the mood for pranks. We don't start the school year off with bad behavior."

One of the gray men was now raising his weapon. And pointing it at me.

"We have to go!" I said. Emily started running. I did too.

But Principal Harker grabbed me by the arm. "I know all the new students. You are not on the list. I think we will be calling the police."

I tried to pull away. Her grip was *tight*. Maybe she was a professional wrestler before she became a principal.

The gray man with the weapon pressed a button, and his flashlight eraser began to shine on my arm. I started to tingle where the light was hitting me. And I could see that part of my body was turning invisible. I couldn't feel or see my hand. My elbow. My arm.

I pulled as hard as I could to get away, but Principal Harker would not let go. She was going to get me killed! The tingling reached my shoulder. The gray man was grinning. Close up, those teeth looked even sharper. And more frightening. And I could just make out his eyes through those sunglasses. They didn't look human.

"The balance has to be restored," the gray man whispered. "Your weight is too much."

That's when piercing bells started ringing all around us.

Principal Harker turned her head. Emily had just yanked one of the fire alarms. I wrenched my arm free and ran past the principal to join Emily. My erased arm was still tingling, but I could see it again. Whew!

I glanced back. Principal Harker was yelling something at us, but the alarm bell was too loud for me to hear what it was. I doubted it was anything positive. The two gray men floated past her. She didn't look their way or stop yelling. Students came tumbling out of the classrooms. One tall boy, no doubt a star player on the basketball team, ran right into one of the gray-suited men and fell over. He stood up and looked all around, everywhere but at the gray man himself.

"No one can see them," I said. "Only us."

"But they can see us," Emily said. "And they want to erase us. We have to get out of here!"

The hallway was jammed with students now. We had to fight our way through the crowd, bumping into backpacks and jostling with what seemed to be half the football team. Then Emily grabbed my hand again and pulled me out of the school.

We ran across the school courtyard and out to the street. There was a three-wheeled city bus waiting there. We hopped on it, and Emily paid our fare and found us a seat near the back.

From the window we could see hundreds of students pouring out of the school. I didn't see the gray men anywhere.

"I think we're safe," I said.

"For now," said Emily. She put her head in her hands. "I just knew something bad was going to happen today."

Twelve

"What do you mean, you *knew*?" I didn't actually ask this question for a couple of minutes. I had to catch my breath first. Then I looked all around the bus to make sure no other gray men were there. The only other person on the bus, besides the bus driver, was an old woman clutching two paper bags stuffed full of groceries.

"Well, I've felt nervous ever since I woke up," said Emily. She moved a lock of hair behind her ear. "And I felt like someone was following me."

Well, technically I had been following her all day.

"No, I don't mean you," she said when she saw my sheepish face. "Looking for me, you know? I just couldn't shake the feeling. And when I told Mick about it, he said he was feeling the same thing. And now these creepy men with razor teeth show up."

"You saw their teeth too?" I asked.

"Yes, and their split tongues. When they spoke."

"Freaky, eh?" I said, because that was all I could think of.

"Freaky and not human," Emily replied. "I've never been as frightened as I was in that classroom."

"You looked brave to me," I said. And I meant it.

She smiled. But only for a second. "Thanks. I didn't feel brave. But once those men showed up, I knew they were the ones who were hunting for me. They came after Mick and me on our way to geometry. So we ducked into that room and, well, you saw the rest."

"Yes, I did," I said. I wanted to get as far away as possible from the men who had erased Mick. I was happy to see the city going by us. We were getting farther and farther away from them. At least, I hoped we were. I stared out the back window, and there weren't any obvious signs of a car following us.

"Isn't it strange what they said?" Emily said.

"That we were overweight?" I said. "It was rude. So rude!"

"That's not how they put it." She looked certain. "They told Mick he weighed too much."

"That's right," I agreed. I liked agreeing with her. "And they said we did too. Then they said—"

"—the balance must be restored." We both said this at the same time.

"Yes!" Emily said. "But what does that mean? Are they crackpots? Why are they talking about weights and balances and things like that?"

"I'm not sure. But I think the words they used are important. They didn't seem angry at us, just logical."

Emily drew in a deep breath. "Michael, can I ask you something?"

"Sure," I said. I knew she probably wasn't going to ask if I wanted to go to a movie.

"What do you think actually happened to Mick? Is he dead?" Emily's chin was wobbling a bit.

"I really don't know," I answered. "Maybe. But we can't know for sure because he just vanished. There weren't even ashes. Or other things left over. Sticky things." My mouth was going faster than my brain again. I looked down at my hand. "I got hit by the flashlight eraser thing too," I said.

"Let's just call it an eraser gun," she said. "What did it feel like?"

"I went all tingly," I said. "I couldn't feel my hand at all. But the feeling in it, and my hand, came back when he stopped pointing the eraser gun at me."

"Maybe Mick isn't gone for good. I hope not. I'm glad you didn't get erased too. I wouldn't want to be figuring this out on my own." She hesitated, like she was going to say something else. Like maybe she liked me? I was pretty sure that was coming next. But instead she said, "It's all so very strange. Two gray men appear, say things about our weight and then point things at us, things that...that erase us. I just don't get it."

"What I want to know is, why doesn't anyone else see them?" I asked.

"That's a really good question," Emily replied. "Mick saw them too," said Emily. "But no one else could. So what's special about us?"

"Well—" I began, then stopped. I didn't know how to say it without being dramatic. "I know what's special about me." She was staring at me like I was the most conceited boy on Earth. Well, Earth Two maybe. I had to explain things quickly. "Remember when I said I was from another universe?"

"I thought you were just joking!" said Emily.

That's when the horrible squealing noise started.

Thirteen

It was from the brakes. The bus was squealing to a halt. I felt a moment of panic. I grabbed the seat in front of me, expecting us to crash. Maybe those gray men were cutting us off?

But it turned out the bus was just old, and this was a routine stop. Another hundred-year-old lady got on and sat down behind the driver. Then the bus started down the street again.

Emily stared at me like I was nuts. "So...about this other-universe thing..."

"Look," I said. "I don't want to freak you out, so I'm just going to tell it to you straight. When I'm done you can decide whether you believe me. But this morning when I work up, I was somewhere very different. Completely different, in fact. I went to my uncle Henry's place. He's a scientist and a math guy. And he was doing this experiment, exploring the theory that one universe might be right next to another."

"The multiverse theory," said Emily.

"Yes," I said, a bit surprised. I liked her even more. "Where universes are lined up like hot dogs on a grill."

"That's an interesting way to put it," she said. "I have always thought of it as eggs next to one another in a pan. Fried eggs."

"Oh, that works too," I said. "Anyway, I ate his chocolate cake. Drank some Dr. Pepper and got a gut ache. When I went to ask him where the antacids were, I stepped in a tin pan full of weighty water."

"Heavy water," she corrected. She really seemed to know this stuff. "And that pan was probably a quantum transporter."

"That's exactly what my uncle called it!" I said. "How do you know so much about this?"

She looked down at her hands and then up at me. "I don't know. But please tell me what happened next. So far you don't sound completely crazy. Just half-crazy."

"Well," I said. "When I stepped into the pan, everything vanished, and I ended up on the street. Here. In your Kingston. Immediately I was almost run over by a three-wheeled car. We mostly have four-wheeled cars on my Earth. Then I jumped to the sidewalk, and that's where I met you."

"Whoa," said Emily. She started rubbing her forehead. "That's quite the story."

"It's not a story." I felt a bit irritated. "It's what happened."

"I'm not trying to call you nuts, Mr. Universe," said Emily. "In fact, I'm pretty sure you're not. But that's a lot to take in."

I liked my new nickname. I was getting to this girl, I just knew it. But she wasn't quite believing me yet. "Here, look at this." I pulled out my phone. The battery was dead. Darn! And there was probably no place in this world that had the right cables for charging it.

Emily took my phone, looked it over and tried to get it to work. Then she handed it back to me.

"That's weird, all right," she said. "Was it a factory mistake? Or some kind of media stunt? The Orange company sometimes does things like that to get attention."

"Where I come from, the company is called Apple," I said.

"Okay, okay," Emily said. "I'm just saying the phone doesn't prove anything."

"You're right," I said. "I can't really prove it."

"It doesn't mean you're not from another universe," Emily said. "But I don't know if there's a way to *prove* you're from another universe."

Then I thought of the gray men. And how they had told both Emily and Mick that they weighed too much. They'd said the same thing to me. But they hadn't seemed concerned about the principal or the other students.

I stared at Emily. "You're from another universe too, aren't you?"

Fourteen

"You're totally bananas," she said. Not in a mean way. But in a surprised way.

Yes, I know what I said sounded crazy. But it also sounded true. I had a gut feeling.

"Why did you say that?" Emily grabbed me by the shoulder. At first I thought she was holding me steady so she could knock me out with a punch. But instead she stared at me intently. "Tell me what you mean."

"Well," I said. The idea had popped into my head, but now I found it hard to expand on it. This was like having the answer to a math problem but not being able to show my work. "Well...I...uh..."

"Explain yourself now!" Emily shook me a little bit. Her fingers were digging into my shoulder. Why was she freaking out like this?

"Well, let's look at the facts," I said. "You just appeared out of nowhere, right?"

"No," she said. "I was found in a library. I didn't just appear there."

"Did anyone see you come in?" I asked.

"No," she said. "But people don't notice everything."

"Librarians do," I said. They certainly notice when books are late. "But let's just say you showed up there."

"Okay," Emily said.

"Well, what if you just showed up because you were *beamed* there?" I said. "Like, transported from another universe?"

"But there's no reason to think that." She still hadn't let go of my shoulder. It was starting to hurt. A lot. "I could easily have banged my head and woken up there."

"Did your head hurt that day?" I asked.

"No."

"And you told me you weren't on any missing-persons list. So..." I pointed my finger up into the air. "Maybe you were sent here."

"Sent?" Her hand squeezed my shoulder even harder.

"Beamed," I said. "Like I was. It explains why the lizard men could see you. And why they could see me and Mick. They are hunting us. But they left everyone else alone. And they yelled at us about our weight."

"They said our weight was unbalanced," she corrected.

"Yes, and I have no idea what that means. But I bet they knew we were from someplace else."

She let go of my shoulder. Ow.

"You know..." Emily took a deep breath. There was a hissing sound behind her. I panicked for a second before I realized it was the bus braking again. "I think you may be right—"

The bus hit something. Hit it very, very hard and came to a screeching halt.

Emily and I didn't come to a halt though. It's science. If something stops suddenly, the things on that something keep going. Emily flew out of our seat and hit the floor. I banged against the seat in front of me.

I got up. Nothing was broken. I went to help Emily, but she was already standing. "Look. We hit a truck," she said. She pointed at the front door of the bus, which had just been yanked open.

Two men in gray suits floated up the steps and down the aisle toward us. They had their eraser guns out.

Fifteen

"Run!" I said. Actually, I may have screamed it. Two or three times.

Emily and I made our way to the very back of the bus. I lifted the emergency-exit bar to unlock the door. We jumped out.

And we started running. Down the street, along the sidewalk and into a park. A woman rolled by on her three-wheeled bicycle, staring. "We need help!"

I shouted. But she just pedaled faster. I glanced back to see the gray men floating from the rear of the bus and down to the ground. They didn't seem to be in a hurry.

I'm not the world's fastest runner. And all I'd had to power my legs that day was chocolate cake, a turkey sandwich and a bottle of Dr. Pepper. I kept racing though.

Emily seemed to be in pretty good shape. She wasn't huffing as much as I was.

"This way," she said and darted down an alley and then turned down another street.

"They seem to be able to track us," I said. "I'm not sure how."

"Then we will have to get really, really far away," said Emily.

I kept thinking about how the gray men were floating. How they didn't tire out. How it seemed they were not going to be stopped.

We needed to go faster.

Which meant we needed something other than a bus. Because they'd obviously tracked it down and caused the crash. But I didn't have any money for a cab.

"Faster," I huffed out. "We need to go faster."

"I can't run much faster," she said.

"I mean with a car. A car."

Then I skidded to a stop.

"What are you doing?" she said, gliding to a stop a few feet ahead of me.

"We need this." I pointed at a parked three-wheeled car and tried the door. It was unlocked. "We have to get away."

I yanked open the door and pulled out my Swiss army knife. Before she could say anything, I had cut a wire or two, hoping that cars here had the same ignition system. I touched the wires together and got a shock. But the motor fired up. "Get in," I said.

"But it's against the law," Emily said.

"It's either take this car or be erased. Which do you choose?"

"Umm...can we say 'borrow the car'?" she asked.

"Yes, that's perfect," I said.

"Good." She opened the glove compartment and got out a piece of paper and a pen. "Don't go yet!"

"What are you doing?"

"I'm just writing a note to the owner," she said. "Saying they'll get the car back, and we'll treat it nicely."

"What? We don't have time."

I looked in the rearview mirror. The gray men had just come out of the alley. They were floating toward us. "Uh, hurry up, Emily!"

"Do you think I should say 'thanks' at the end? Or 'sorry'?" she asked.

"Both," I said. "Just write it."

The gray men were now only about thirty feet behind us.

"Okay, done," she said. She opened the door and dropped the note on the ground. "Let's go."

We both did up our seat belts. I flipped the signal light on, then pulled out into the street.

And then I stepped on the gas.

I could see the gray men lifting their eraser guns. Maybe they could somehow stop the car. Or erase us while we were driving.

So I cranked the wheel and sped down an alley. I raced away as fast as I dared.

"Where are we going?" Emily asked after a few minutes.

"I don't know," I said. "This isn't my Earth." But then I remembered something really important. "Actually, I know exactly where we need to go."

Sixteen

It turned out this Kingston was almost exactly like my Kingston. And it also turned out I could steer a three-wheeled car quite well. It handled great, though I felt weird knowing there was only one wheel at the front. I kept expecting the car to flip over. But it stayed balanced.

I turned onto the main drag, Central Street, and went just a pinch over the speed limit. We passed a

McGregor's and a Jim Hortons. I remembered I was hungry.

And that I was in a different world.

"We need to figure out how they were able to track us," Emily said.

"They might have seen us get on the bus."

"Maybe," she said. "But we have to assume they somehow always know where we are. Maybe those eraser guns can smell us."

"Smell us?" I repeated. I was happy to see we were leaving the downtown core and getting into a part of the city where there were mostly houses. They looked just like the houses on my Earth. Except their front doors were round. It made me think of the houses in that movie with hobbits in it.

"Well, I don't know if *smell* is the right word," Emily said. "Maybe it's our brainwaves that they… they sense."

"You're probably right," I said. "So no matter where we go, they might eventually find us."

"I don't want to keep running the rest of my life," she said.

"Me either. Plus, we don't have enough gas to do that." I looked for a gas gauge but couldn't find one. "Assuming this runs on gas."

"Actually, it's hydrogen-powered," she said.

"Oh, wow," I said. "That explains why it's so quiet. Umm, you don't happen to have another turkey sandwich on you, do you?"

"No, I don't," she said. "I gave the other one to Mick, and he…" She made a sound almost like a sob. I glanced over at her. She looked very sad. I had to remember that she had seen her friend get erased earlier that day. I mean, I'd been freaked out enough myself just seeing it. She'd actually known him.

I took one hand off the wheel. Well, I unclamped it because I was driving kind of nervous-like. I patted her shoulder. "It'll be okay," I said.

"I don't know about that," she said. "But I think I need to close my eyes for a bit."

And she did. I don't know if she slept, but I drove keeping one eye on the rearview mirror. We were soon out of Kingston. I turned onto one of the less busy highways and kept driving. There were fewer and fewer houses now, and eventually there were just big fields and small farmyards.

When I went down a gravel road, the car started to really shake, and Emily opened her eyes and yawned. "Where are we?" she asked.

"Just one second," I said. The road was really familiar. So were the oak trees. I made one more turn, and now we were driving straight toward a house.

A familiar dome house. "Welcome to my uncle Henry's house," I said. "I'm hoping he can save us."

Seventeen

"This isn't really your uncle's house, is it?" Emily asked when we got out of the car. We started walking toward the front door. Like all the other doors in this world, it was circular. "Someone entirely different could be living here. And they might not like trespassers."

"Only my uncle would build a dome house," I said. "It looks almost exactly like the one I've spent so much time at—except for this round door." I pointed at the smaller dome on top of the house, with the telescope sticking out of it. "That's even the same telescope. If anyone will believe our story, it will be Uncle Henry. I mean, he's the one who sent me here, right? So maybe *this* Uncle Henry is doing the exact same experiment and can help us."

"But the person in this house won't even know you," said Emily. "In fact, there might not even be anyone like you on this planet." She looked at me. "Actually, I'm pretty sure of that."

"What do you mean?" I asked. It didn't sound like she was being sarcastic. I wondered if she meant it as compliment.

"You're one of a kind," she said. "If I have to hang out with someone while I'm being chased by men in gray suits, I'm glad it's you."

I nearly blushed. "Well, thanks. Let's see if my Earth Two uncle is home."

I knocked. The door opened. And my jaw dropped.

Standing in front of me was a woman. Uncle Henry had been a bachelor all his life, but in this world he'd found a wife. My mom would be so amazed! And happy for him.

"Michael!" she said. And she grabbed me and pulled me into a bear hug, squeezing hard enough to knock the breath out of my lungs. Then she pushed me away from her but kept her hands on my shoulders. "I thought you were in Europe with your parents!"

"I was in Europe?" I said, shocked. "Wow. And my parents took me? You mean, they're still together?"

She raised an eyebrow. The movement seemed very familiar. Had Uncle Henry married someone I knew?

"Of course they are! A six-month tour of Europe—a family trip. You're missing school and everything."

"I'm missing six months of school?" I nearly shouted this. "That sounds like heaven!"

She raised her other eyebrow. Now I knew who she reminded me of.

Uncle Henry. Same nose. And those elf-like ears. On this planet, my uncle Henry was an aunt.

"When did you get back?" she asked. "Is everything okay? Why didn't your mom phone me?" Then she looked over my shoulder to where Emily was standing "And who's this girl?"

"Oh," I said. The woman who looked like my uncle finally let me go. I stepped back a bit to point a thumb at Emily. "This is my friend Emily. Emily, this is my...my..." I didn't know what to say.

"Ignore him," the woman said. She stuck out her hand, and Emily shook it. "I'm his aunt, Henrietta. Everyone calls me Henry."

"Aunt Henry," I stuttered. "I have an aunt Henry?"

"Have you been drinking Red Bill?" Aunt Henry asked. "Or too much fizzy Croke?"

"No," I said. "I'm just a little light-headed today. And I—"

She suddenly reached out and pushed back the hair from my forehead. "Hey! Where is it?"

"Where is what?" I asked.

"The scar on your forehead. The one I call your Barry Potter scar. You got it from falling in my workroom and hitting a microscope. Your mom wouldn't let you visit me for months after that. Where is it?"

"Oh, um, Aunt, um, Henry," I said. I took a deep breath. "You might find a few things are different about me. You see, I've traveled back from, well, from—"

"From a bit farther away than Europe," Emily said, rescuing me. "And we'd like to tell you about it. Is it okay if we come inside?"

Eighteen

We followed Aunt Henry into a dome home that looked exactly like Uncle Henry's. There was even a collection of toy robots like his, and the same ratty couch. Even the tube TV on a table in the corner looked just like my uncle's. We sat on the couch and Aunt Henry brought us some tea, which she'd just made.

"No Dr. Pepper?" I asked. "Or Dr. Who?"

"What's a Dr. Pepper?" Aunt Henry said. "Or a Dr. Who?"

"Oh, it's just a joke," I said. "Never mind."

She did Uncle Henry's raised-eyebrow thing again. It was freaky to look at. "So, Michael, you and your friend have a story to tell," she said. "Why don't you start?"

I thought it best to jump right in. "I'm from another Earth," I said. "Like a multiverse Earth. Hot Dog One," I said. "You sent me here."

"This is not funny, Michael," Aunt Henry said.

"It's not a joke," Emily said. "He's just nervous." She reached over and patted my hand. Immediately I calmed down. "We've had a lot happen today. Maybe Michael can start from the beginning and tell you the whole thing. Then you can ask questions."

Aunt Henry nodded. I should point out that she wasn't bald like Uncle Henry. Her red hair was styled in a messy bun. Now that I thought about it, pictures from my parents' wedding showed that Uncle Henry once had red hair.

I took a deep breath. And I began telling the story. I didn't skip anything. I even mentioned the chocolate cake and how *she* was a *he* on the other Earth. How I'd stepped into the shallow pan full of water and ended up on Earth Two. And that now we were being chased by men in gray suits with sharp, sharp teeth. I covered the part about "borrowing" a car really, really quickly. "And then we drove here," I said. I sat back with a big sigh.

The whole time I spoke, Aunt Henry nodded, but her face didn't show whether she thought we were nuts. Or crazy. Or even if she believed us. It was the perfect poker face.

"So what do you think?" I asked.

"I believe you," she said.

"You do?" Emily said. "Why?"

Aunt Henry stood up. She went over to the kitchen and opened the fridge.

She came back in with a chocolate cake covered in chocolate icing. One slice had been cut out of it. "Because of this," she said. "There was no way for you to know there was a chocolate cake in my fridge."

I let out my breath. I hadn't realized I'd been holding it for so long. "So what do we do now?" I asked.

"We have some cake!" she said. She put it down and sliced it. She handed us each a piece on a plate. "And I'm going to get something a bit stronger than tea."

She came back with a big bottle of Croke. She didn't offer us any. I dug into my piece of cake. It tasted just like cake.

It tasted so good I may have had another piece.

"You're definitely related to my nephew," Aunt Henry said. "He'd eat that whole cake in a heartbeat."

"I did that a few hours ago," I said. "I'd like to meet him."

"I'm not sure how that would go," Aunt Henry said. "I think he might freak out. Your mom—I mean, his mom—certainly would."

"So what do you think we should do?" Emily asked. She glanced over her shoulder. And I knew what she was thinking. We had driven more than an hour away from the city. But the gray men would find us sooner or later.

"Let me see that phone," Aunt Henry said. I handed it to her, and she looked it up and down. "Whoa, that is a weird plug-in. But I think I can figure out a way to charge it." She got up, went to a messy worktable and sorted through a tangle of cords there. She plugged one end of a cord into a wall outlet and then plugged the other end into the phone. "Eureka!" she said. "So volts work the same in our worlds. I was worried I'd blow up your phone."

I nearly spit out my tea.

Aunt Henry sat down again. It was impossible to not think of her as my actual aunt. She finished off her glass of Croke and refilled it. "So you said you could call your uncle on that phone?"

"Yes," I said.

"Well, we may have to do that," she said.

"But we've come to the right place, haven't we?" I asked. "I mean, you must be working on a pan of weighty water that takes us to another universe, right? So you can send me and maybe Emily back to my Earth. We'd be safe there."

Aunt Henry shook her head. "No. Sorry. I don't like tiny science."

"Tiny science?" Emily asked.

"Yeah, quantum stuff. It's looking at small things. Like the insides of molecules. I like big things. Moons. Planets. Black holes. Wormholes. In fact, a wormhole would be really handy right now."

"Oh," I said. "So are you saying that you can't help us?"

"Well, I don't have a wormhole in my back pocket," she said. Smiling. "Good thing, because who knows where my pants would end up?" She laughed, staring at us like she expected us to laugh too. But I didn't get the joke and was too nervous to fake a laugh.

"You and my uncle have the same sense of humor," I said.

"I will take that as a compliment," Aunt Henry said. "I do have good news. I paid attention in class. So I understand what your uncle was trying to do. Wait—what he *succeeded* in doing when he sent you here." She pointed at Emily. "Though I don't know how to explain you."

"I do feel like I'm from somewhere else," Emily said.

"We all do," Aunt Henry said. "It's human nature. Now tell me about these gray guys."

"Gray lizard men," I corrected.

"Yes, tell me what they said to you." Aunt Henry crossed her arms. "Exactly. I think their words matter."

We told her.

Aunt Henry still had her arms crossed. "So it seems they want everything to be balanced."

"Yes," Emily said.

"*Adjustments are required*," Aunt Henry said. "Were they angry when they said it?"

"No," Emily said. "They seemed calm. Like they just had a job to do."

"Let me think on that for a second." Aunt Henry took a sip of Croke. "Have some more cake."

I didn't want to say that I'd throw up if I had any more. But I finished the last of my tea.

"I've got it!" Emily said. She even had one finger in the air.

Aunt Emily and I both stared at her.

"I think I know what those freaks meant when they were talking about balance," Emily said. "There's this theory that after the Big Bang there was a set amount of matter in the universe. An exact amount allotted. Not a molecule more."

"Not everyone follows that theory," Aunt Henry said. "But I see where you're going with this."

I had no idea where Emily was going or how she knew this stuff.

"It must mean we weigh too much for this world," Emily said.

"What?" I said.

"Bingo," Aunt Henry said.

They actually gave each other a high five.

"I am not following you," I said. I didn't like feeling stupid. But this was a bad time to pretend I understood. "What do you mean?"

"Well, it's like this," Emily said. "The gray men erased Mick and want to erase you and me because our weight is from another universe. That puts this universe out of balance."

"I'm still not sure I get it," I said. But I was starting to understand a little.

"The gray men are like border guards," Emily said. "They chased us down because we aren't supposed to be here. We make this universe weigh more. So they have to erase us."

"Okay," I said. "But when they erase us, do we just vanish? Or do we go somewhere else?"

We all looked at each other. I thought it was kind of an important question.

"I don't know," Aunt Henry said. "But I bet I know who does. Get your uncle on the phone."

Nineteen

"Michael!" my uncle said. "You're alive!"

"Yes," I said. His face was on my phone—I was FaceTiming him. From Earth Two to Earth One. No idea how that could be possible, but we didn't have a lot of time to analyze. "I'll explain later. There's someone here I want you to talk to." I handed the phone to Aunt Henry.

"Hello, Uncle Henry," she said. "It's Aunt Henry on the line."

My uncle's eyes were as big as eggs. He was in total shock. Then he said a quiet, "Hello. It's nice to meet you."

"We have some figuring out to do," Aunt Henry said. And that is when they started talking nonstop. Using a billion fancy words. Big ones. Small ones. They both talked so quickly that I couldn't keep track. I did catch Aunt Henry saying something about a wormhole in her pocket. My uncle laughed his guts out.

"They seem to be two of a kind," Emily said.

"Yep, they sure are," I agreed.

Finally Aunt Henry handed me the phone. My uncle waved. He sure looked happy.

"Follow me into my workshop," Aunt Henry said.

We practically ran there. I propped the phone on a table, and Uncle Henry began shouting orders.

And Aunt Henry shouted orders too. Emily and I followed them, grabbing glass tubes, old lightbulbs and wires and bringing them to the main worktable. We started to put together something that looked a little like the crazy device I'd seen in my uncle's lab. We must have used the parts from at least five computers. And a hundred little wires. Emily was really good with a soldering gun. I was good with electronics—I knew how to plug things in.

We worked fast. We worked hard. I started to sweat.

Finally Aunt Henry put down a pan of water a lot like the one I'd stepped into what seemed like years ago. She connected some wires to it, measured something and then sighed. "Listen," she said. "These wires are the wrong grade. I need to go out to the garage. I'll be right back."

She rushed out of the room.

"How are you doing?" Uncle Henry asked from the tiny screen.

"I'm okay. I'm a little worried about those gray men," I admitted.

"I learned a bit more about them," he said. "I reached out to some of my scientist friends. The gray men are from a group that goes from universe to universe making sure the wrong people aren't in the wrong universe. They've even been on our Earth."

"They have?" I said. "So other people have visited our world?"

"Yes. And my scientists have encountered these custodians."

"Custodians," Emily said. "You mean they're like janitors?"

"Yes," Uncle Henry said. "That's a good way to think of them. They clean things up. We don't know where they came from. But they are ruthless at their job. They will do anything to get a universe's balance back."

"You tried to warn me about them before," I said.

"Yes, I did," he said. "I'd just heard about them on the interwebs." He's always said *interwebs* instead of *internet*. I don't know why. "But once we get you back here, you'll be safe. Everything will be in balance."

"Whew!" I said. Then I looked at Emily. "What about Emily? Will *she* be safe?"

"Well..." Uncle Henry said. "I have two pieces of bad news. I did some math. The first thing is that if Emily comes to our Earth, the custodians will follow her."

"So there's no place she can hide?" I said. "Can she go back to her own world?" Not that I wanted her to do that. I really wanted her to be in a place I could visit. Maybe we actually could go to a movie. Or eat another turkey sandwich together.

"Well, that's the other bad news," my uncle said. "You see, Emily isn't real."

"What do you mean she's not real?" I poked Emily with a finger.

"Cut that out!" she said.

"She's right here, Uncle Henry," I said. I was holding my arm now because she'd pinched me back. Hard.

"No, I put that wrong," Uncle Henry said. "She's real right now. But she wasn't real before she got transported to that world."

"Please explain what you mean," Emily said.

"She came from a lab," Uncle Henry said. "Just like my lab. Except the person who tried to go to Earth Two sent a copy of themselves there."

"You mean she's a copy of someone else?" I asked.

"Yes," Uncle Henry said. "That person stayed in the other world. Her world. And sent her. They probably don't know that she's going to be erased. The same thing with your friend Mick. It's called the 'twin effect.' I wrote a paper on it. I'm so glad to know my math was right."

"Yeah, congrats, Uncle." I couldn't hide my sarcasm.

"I'm sorry," he said. "And I know for you, Emily, this is very strange. I'm sorry to be the bearer of bad news."

"It's okay," she said. She sounded brave. "Really, it is. It explains so much about the things I feel. And where I came from. Thank you. It's better for me to know this, right?" Then she drew in a deep breath. "So there really isn't a universe for me?"

"No, there isn't," he said. He sounded very sad. I know I *felt* very sad. I put my hand on Emily's. She was real. She was right there.

We were all silent for several seconds.

"Dangnabbit!" Uncle Henry said. He had weird swear words. "There must be a way to solve this. It's *FFHHDNZZZ.*"

"What?" I said.

"*Frzzzgh,*" my uncle said. The phone was buzzing like mad now. His image was fading in and out. "*Frrzzegh izz.*"

"We can't hear you!" I shouted.

"Just don't *FFFRGHS.*"

Then the phone stopped buzzing. The battery was dead. What horrible timing!

But it turned out it was a good thing.

Because once the phone stopped buzzing, I could hear a new sound. A motor. "Oh no," I said. "They're here."

I ran to the window. There was only one car in the driveway. Ours. Emily was looking out the other window. "No one there," she said.

"But we both heard a vehicle, right?" I said.

She nodded.

The door to the lab suddenly banged open. We both jumped straight up in the air.

"What's wrong?" Aunt Henry asked. She was holding a handful of wires. "You two look like you've seen a ghost."

Twenty

"I'm sorry to hear that, Emily," Aunt Henry said once we'd caught her up. "I'll keep you safe as long as I can. The good news is, I've got all the right wires. It's going to take me a few minutes to rewire the pan. Maybe those noises were nothing. I didn't see anyone outside."

Which is when we heard something hit the roof. Then something else hit it. There was a skylight above us. Through it I could see a helicopter with three rotors floating up there.

Two men in gray came into view. They looked down at us through the skylight.

"They've found us!" I said, stating the obvious. "They're here!"

Aunt Henry looked up, stared, but didn't say anything for a few seconds. "Huh. I really can't see them," she said. "Just like you said."

"They are there," Emily said. "I don't think you have time to do the wiring."

Aunt Henry tossed me a brown box. "You're going to have to distract them."

"What is it?" I said.

"Something I was working on in the garage," she said.

I looked at the device. It had one big button on it. "It looks like a garage-door opener."

"It's not," Aunt Henry said. "It's an atomic scrambler."

"What does it do?" Emily asked.

"It will send a signal. Kind of like the ones you must be sending them right now. I think they'll be attracted to it."

The custodians were trying to pry open the skylight. It started to creak.

"Well, isn't that something," Aunt Henry said. "It's like invisible hands are opening my skylight." And then she whispered, "Both of you, run. See that tree all by itself at the end of the yard? That's where I have my outdoor cellar. Go there. Get out of their line of sight and throw that box as far as you can into the trees. Once you're in the cellar, you'll find a tunnel back to the house. I had it built in case there's a World War Four. I hope it hasn't collapsed."

"Collapsed?" I said. That did not sound safe.

"Yes," Aunt Henry said. "Go now!" She patted my shoulder.

Emily and I ran from the house, not even pausing to close the door.

The cellar looked like it was a football field away. Why hadn't she built it closer? When we were about halfway to it, I glanced over my shoulder.

The custodians were floating down from the roof. And coming toward us. They seemed to be picking up speed. I figured they had more than one gear.

"Faster!" I shouted. "They're gaining on us."

It turned out we both had another gear too. We made it to the cellar. I had to stop for a second to catch my breath.

"Throw the scrambler," Emily said.

"I will!" I said. "I just need a moment."

"We don't have time! They're almost here. Throw it now!"

So I threw the thing. It was heavy, but I must say I made a pretty great throw. Any outfielder or quarterback would be proud to make that kind of throw.

Then I turned and put my hand on the cellar door. It was locked.

"Oh no," I whispered. "It's locked."

"Can't you unlock it?" Emily hissed. "Twist it. Keep trying. They're getting closer."

Then she hugged me.

Well, she pushed me against the door.

"Don't move," she whispered.

The custodians went straight toward where I'd thrown the brown box. They floated right past us, into the forest and out of sight.

The cellar door opened under our weight, and we tumbled down a set of stairs. I got up to close the door, glancing out at the trees. There was no sign of the custodians. I went back down the stairs.

Then we ran, past the potatoes and onions and into a long tunnel. It was dark, but Emily got out her round phone and used it as a flashlight. There were a million spiderwebs, but the tunnel hadn't collapsed.

It seemed to take forever, but we made it back to the house. We climbed a set of stairs and opened a trapdoor. We were in the lab again.

Aunt Henry was right there to help us out. "Good work," she said. "The transporter is ready."

Twenty-One

"Quick," she said. She started flicking switches, and a bunch of colored buttons on the transport device came on. Lights in the house dimmed. This gadget was draining the whole place of electricity.

"Everything is ready," said Aunt Henry. "If your uncle's math is correct, and I'm sure it is because I've checked it twice, this should send you back to your

Earth, Michael. Back to safety. Once you're gone, I'll take Emily in my car and we'll run. To NASO. I know a couple of quantum physicists there who may be able to help us."

"Oh," I said. "Okay."

"Stand in the pan," Aunt Henry said. She pointed. Maybe she didn't think I knew what a pan was.

I looked at Emily. I didn't know what to say. How do you say goodbye to a girl who gave you a turkey sandwich? "I don't know what to say," I said.

"I do," Emily said. "Thanks for everything, Michael. You're great. I really like you. And good luck in your universe."

"Thanks," I said. "Um...same to you." I reached out to pat her shoulder, but she gave me a hug.

"Now go!" she commanded.

I stepped into the pan. I looked back at Emily. It was the last time I would ever see her.

"Three, two, one," Aunt Henry said. "Transport!"

She flicked a switch. At that exact moment, the whole house went dark.

I didn't go anywhere. There was just the sound of the transporter powering down.

"Did we blow a breaker?" I asked.

"No," she said. "Someone cut the outdoor lines."

Which is when a sharp-toothed custodian blasted in through the door of the lab. The other custodian came out of the open trapdoor. They had taken off their sunglasses, and this time they didn't look calm. They looked angry.

I could see it in their glowing lizard eyes.

"They're here!" Emily said. "One at the door. The other coming out the trapdoor. And they're moving fast!" Why was she shouting out the obvious? Then I realized she was letting Aunt Henry know what was going on.

Aunt Henry swung a broom. "I can't see them. Did I hit one?" she asked.

"You're not even close," I said. I stepped out of the transporting pan, but Emily immediately shoved me right back in.

"I'll lead them away," Emily said. "Your aunt can get the power going."

"No," I said.

She grabbed me by the shoulder and looked me right in the eye. "It only makes sense, Michael. I have no other world to go to. One of us should live. Let me delay them and…"

The lights started to come back on.

"The generator kicked in!" Aunt Henry said. "Great!" She swung her broom again and this time connected with one of the custodians. His eraser gun flew across the room. "I got one. I think I got one!" She swung again and knocked him back.

But the other custodian was now right in front of Emily and me.

"Come and get me," Emily shouted.

Then she started to run away. Away from the custodian. Away from me.

The custodian pointed his eraser gun at her.

I grabbed Emily's right hand and yanked her back with all my strength. When she realized what was happening, she started pulling back. "Stop it, Michael! Let me go."

"No," I said. "There's another way."

But I was too late. She was starting to get erased. First her left arm. Then her shoulder. "It tingles," she said. "It tingles. Goodbye, Michael."

But I grabbed at the eraser gun too. Now I was pulling on both Emily and the hand of the custodian. He turned his lizard eyes on me.

He blinked sideways. Not up and down like humans do. So creepy!

"We must balance everything," he said in a flat voice. "Everything must return to normal."

But I didn't let go. I shouted, "Send me home! Send me home!"

"Good luck!" Aunt Henry said, and she hit some switch with her broomstick. The machine burped electricity that shot through my feet and right though me. I began to tingle.

But I held on as tightly as I could.

With both hands.

Twenty-Two

There was darkness. Then spinning lights. Then more darkness.

Now I was ankle deep in the same pan of water. In the same room. It hadn't worked!

"Oh no!" I shouted.

Then I looked up. Uncle Henry was standing there with a great big smile on his face. The biggest one I'd ever seen. "I can't believe it worked!" he said.

"You didn't think it would?" I asked.

"I didn't get a chance to double-check my math." He glanced to my right. "Is this Emily?"

And that's when I became aware that I was holding on to something with my right hand. Emily's hand. And Emily was attached to the rest of it. All of her! I hadn't left a single piece of her behind.

"Are you okay?" I asked.

"Yes," she said. "Yes. You...you brought me through."

"I guess I did," I said.

"Yeah, I hadn't calculated for two people," Uncle Henry said. "But math can be tricky. I'm so glad you two didn't switch brains. So what's that?"

He was indicating my other hand. I was almost afraid to look, in case I was still clutching the custodian. But it was only the eraser gun. "It's one of the gray men's machines," I said. "It erases people." I saw that there were little bulbous sacks at the end of the gun. I poked one, and it fell to the floor. Oops.

"Oh," Uncle Henry said. "So that's what they do."

I stepped out of the pan and onto solid ground. I let go of Emily's hand. She rubbed it. "Sorry," I said. "I didn't mean to squeeze so hard."

"I'm glad you did," she said. "Otherwise, I might not be here."

"Yes, it's great," I said. "But...we have a problem, don't we?"

"Yes," she said. "The custodians will be looking for me."

"That's right," Uncle Henry said. "They will. In fact, I'm guessing they'll be here—"

A green light began to shine in the middle of the room. It opened into a round, shining hole.

"Oh, they're here," my uncle said.

"Already?" Emily said. "I just got here."

"Well, they have your readings," Uncle Henry said. He sounded really calm. I could see a figure in the green circle, a bit far away as if it were coming down a tunnel. It was definitely a custodian. Another one was right behind him.

"So yeah," Uncle Henry said. "They can find you. And they can move from universe to universe very quickly."

"Why do you sound so calm?" I asked.

The custodians had reached the end of their green tunnel. They were now coming through. My uncle had put on a pair of green glasses that had been lying on the table. "So that's what they look like," he said. "This is exciting. I really wanted to see them."

"But what about Emily?" I asked.

The first custodian out of the tunnel looked at me. He turned away—I was nothing. I was in the right universe. And then he looked at Emily.

"This is what I was trying to explain on the phone," said Uncle Henry. "I may have figured out a way to solve this." He lifted up what looked like a hand vacuum.

He touched Emily's head with it, and a gauge popped up from the device. Then he flicked a switch and pointed the thing at his workbench and sucked up several glass objects. And metal bolts. And a book or two. Then he flicked another switch. The machine whined for a second and stopped.

"You're cleaning your house? Now?" I asked.

The custodians were on either side of Emily. One had his eraser gun pointed at her.

He was going to erase Emily.

I was just about to jump when I noticed something.

The custodian wasn't erasing her. He had a strange look on his face. Like he was confused.

He shook his device. He sniffed. He looked from me to my uncle to Emily. "The balance is restored," he said. He turned away from us, and he and his partner stepped back into the green tunnel. It closed up behind them.

They were gone.

"I'm going to live?" Emily said.

"Of course," Uncle Henry answered. "Math solves all problems."

"What did you do?" I asked.

"Oh, I weighed her with this." He pointed at the gauge. "Right down to the atom. Then I sucked the same amount of weight off my desk. I had preprogrammed this to send that matter to another universe. One that is dead so it won't cause any problems. And then everything was in balance again. Like I said, math solves all problems."

We stared at him. He leaned down, picked up a six-pack of soda from the floor and offered us one. "Dr. Pepper?"

"Yes," I said. "For both of us."

So Emily got her very first taste of Dr. Pepper. "Well, I could get used to this," she said. Then she let out a sigh. "I—I do wish Mick could have been saved. I feel bad about him. If only we'd known about that vacuum trick of yours. He was a nice guy."

"Oh, he can be saved," Uncle Henry said.

"You mean he could have been saved," I said. "I'm pretty sure that's what you mean."

Uncle Henry reached into his pocket and pulled out the bulb thing that I had knocked off the eraser gun. "I noticed this alien container on the floor. And I realized something. They weren't going to erase you. They would have put you into a non-mass container pod."

"Huh?" I said.

"Your friend is in here." Uncle Henry tapped on the bulb container. "It'll take me a while to figure out how to get him out. But he's perfectly fine. And then, if he wants to stay in our world, it's just a matter of doing the same calculations I did for Emily."

"Oh," I said. "That's great news." Although maybe not for me. I still hadn't figured out whether Emily had a thing for him.

"It might take me a year or so," Uncle Henry said. "But he won't notice. I suspect time isn't a factor in this pod."

"Thank you so much," Emily said. She gave my uncle a hug. "I'm glad Mick is going to be okay.

He is a really nice guy. I mean, not as nice as Michael here, who saved my life a few times."

I blushed. "Don't forget you saved mine too."

"So," Uncle Henry said as he pointed at Emily, "we just have to figure out where you'll live. And find you a family too. I have contacts in the secret parts of the government who will help. We'll get you settled. Now, would anyone like some cake?"

Twenty-Three

My mom and Dad Two were surprised when they came to pick me up. Not surprised to see me, because they had no idea I'd been to another universe. And I wasn't about to tell them. They would have never let me visit my uncle again.

They were surprised to see Emily though. I told them that Emily was visiting from next door. Mom looked at Emily. She looked at me. I knew *she* knew

I had a thing for Emily. She smiled, and her eyes twinkled. But whatever. They waited in the car while I said goodbye.

"Well, see you around, I guess." I was back to not having anything clever to say.

"Wait a second." Emily pulled out her round phone and looked at it. "Whoa. It still works," she said. "Text me when you get home."

"I will," I promised.

As soon I got home I texted her.

Are you busy this weekend? Want to see a movie?

Emily answered immediately.

Sure! In this universe? Or another one? LOL

Arthur Slade is a Governor General's Award–winning author of many novels for young readers, including the Amber Fang series and *Death by Airship* from the Orca Currents line. Raised on a ranch in the Cypress Hills of Saskatchewan, Arthur now makes his home in Saskatoon.